Jarr Darr

Love to Grave

Part 1 of 3

Contents of all three parts:

1. Singles city

2. Single game in Pairs

3. Sarah

4. A quiet evening with the

armrest in the background

5. The power of sexy on one

6. The course at 13:45 did not take place

7. Sara vs Kari. Someone has to go

8. Demons of the past

9. Demon number 2

10. Drunken Park

11. Cecylia Lassic

12. Feminium

13. One, two, three, four and

five, you die

1. Singles city

Frank Mauser took a seat by the window of the cruise bus to begin his journey to his destiny. However, destiny caught up with him sooner. In the form of a mature woman walking towards him inside the bus.

From nowhere, memories of Frank's teenage years came with her. When it was at the end of the semester, after successfully passing another school subject, he ran out of school, catching a bus.

He was in a rush to get home, where an indecently pleasant surprise awaited him.

In the crowded vehicle, the deliberations on the meaning of existence were interrupted by another stop, where the pressure of passengers threw Frank deep into the crackling of the old vehicle.

Grabbing the handrail, he landed smoothly, brushing gracefully against the woman in front of him, who was bravely clutching the same handrail as he was.

The curly red hair of an unfamiliar woman, stroking his face, caused more and more warmth covering subsequent parts of the young man's body. How many turns and rocking could he endure in adolescence, feeling the sexy body of a mature, charming woman, rubbing against him every now and then to the rhythm of the bus swaying through city streets?

Finally, he rudely surrendered to the moment with the woman. She too was hungry for pleasure with the young man. She felt Eros' arrow dig into her body, along with the young man's cock sticking out. He pressed harder and harder against her skirt, tautening it mercilessly. Kissing the woman's hair, he touched her hand. He felt the firmness of his buttocks, stimulating yet inexperienced masculinity. The passenger was rocking her hips more and more, warming the boy up even more, wanting to even bite him with her buttocks. His penis tried to pierce his pants, tucking the short skirt into the woman's anal pass, inviting him to explore.

Young Frank's solid cock, stretched to the breaking point, wanted to jump out and penetrate new spaces. As the bus ran trembling on the tram rails, Frank felt that he was losing control of the situation and the fuse in the cannon was burning before firing.

Suddenly, the mysterious woman shattered Frank's memories by asking:

- Is this seat taken?

"But of course, go ahead," he said, taking his hand luggage from the armchair next to him.

- No ... Not that. I meant the window seat.

- The window seat is in front of me or in the back! Frank replied.

"But I want by the window next to you ..." She whispered loudly and coquettishly, leaning over the man.

The woman presented the advantages of a deep neckline and cut-outs in the skirt that allowed you to see the garter. Under the pressure of arguments of her femininity, he moved to the second seat, intrigued by the directness of the woman. The one with cat dexterity sat down in the place she had acquired. He must already envy the armchair that hugs me so tenderly, she thought contemptuously of the entire male species, so susceptible to sensual manipulation.

The appearance of the strange fellow passenger had questioned the meaning of Frank's hardened, lonely existence. And yet there are women who can surprise! He thought, and something was starting to happen in his pants.

Despite Thor's appealing physiognomy from the Marvel comics, he failed to attract this true other half. Perhaps it was his complicated nature that did not allow it? Certainly the work of a personal bodyguard did not help.

Admiring the woman's supremely alluring legs, he heard:

- Did you spot anything interesting?

Unmasked, he replied:

- I contemplate the surface tension of the stockings on your calves.

- And what? It's good? She asked with a smile and flirtatiously narrowed eyes.

- It's hard to say without the use of tactile technique.

Without saying anything, the woman lifted her foot and slipped it into the linen leg of his trousers, caressing the man tenderly.

- And now? She asked after a moment.

- Perfect. He put a hand on the stranger's knee and felt the warmth emanating from the inside of her thighs.

Plunging his gaze into the brown of the woman's narrowed eyes, he ran his hand around her, lovingly caressing both of her calves. As he slipped his hand bit by bit farther and farther, he was gaining new territory under her leather skirt. Halfway to the delightful triangle, she grabbed his hand. She brought her mouth to Frank's ear and asked:

- Who are you, you bastard?

Sliding his hand into black hairstyles travel female comrades, he sank his lips in her ear, whispering tenderly:

- I'm a contraceptive test tester.

He kissed the area of the earring with small, tender kisses. Across his neck, he reached the other ear and asked:

- And who are you?

"Exciting inspiration from the past, nightmare of the future," she said mysteriously.

- And in the present? - He did not give up, not fully understanding the meaning of the statement.

"Myself," she cut short the discussion, harassing

his swollen genitalia.

The bus was entering the Desire Station. Frank felt the woman's soft lips. First, a careful hug. Then the warmth of her breath against his cheek. More and more intense gaze, filled with eroticism.

His tongue asked for entrance. She opened her mouth slightly. He brushed her lips lightly, then slipped smoothly inside. It met her thirsty tongue. The two tongues clasped together like a couple dancing wildly on the dance floor of their mouths. She released his hand, caught earlier, and opened her legs slightly. The woman allowed him to gain her most sensitive areas. At the same time, she deftly released Frank's erect penis outside. She was playing with it vigorously. She was driving him crazy. During this time, she was explored deeper and more boldly by a man. He sank with delight in her moist vagina.

The buttons on her blouse and bra gave way to the pressure of lust. He revealed the magnificent breasts of a woman with sexily protruding nipples burning with desire. They wanted a caress. At that moment, his tongue began to dance eagerly. He made her nipples moist by walking around them. His mobility gave the woman piercing pleasure. Extremely exciting grip of the mouth, it entwined the nipples of the woman from all sides.

He ran his lips in kisses all over the spherical surface of her breast.

The woman returned the caresses. She tugged and scratched him. Reaching for a hard cock, she did not forget about the captivating caress with her lips. She brought the penis to the end of its endurance. Sitting down on the naughty phallus, she caught it all in her female snares. Stuffing herself deeply on the penis, she consumed with her predatory vagina, appetizing and throbbing penis in it. Swaying, she rolled her hips in all directions. She made the man completely submissive.

Frank's hands were running all over the body of an amazing brunette driving her to ecstasy. He was madly kissing her sexy body, every place he got. He writhed under her with delight.

She pressed him tightly against her. In a broken, shaky voice, she whispered:

- Your lockpick broke all my contraceptive precautions, let it be now!

He did not stand it. He exploded profusely in the woman. Sighing, they drowned in ecstatic orgasm.

***

They arrived at their destination in the morning. Richer for a new acquaintance, they parted in their respective directions.

It was surprising for Frank that the person who was picked up by the limousine with the driver was traveling in the bus crowd. However, people have different needs and preferences, so he quickly stopped thinking about it.

Retaining some of her hair on his sweater, he took a taxi to his new apartment. However, he had the strange belief that this was not his first meeting with this woman. Frank felt it might not be the last either.

***

In appearance, Singles City was similar to other

concrete cities. However, it made a positive first impression. By exploring its secrets more, you could see the not very family nature of this place. Promiscuity was not particularly stigmatized. People lived here mainly in open relationships. Frank's apartment was located in a long, atmospheric building surrounded by park greenery. The windows overlooked both sides of the building, thanks to which the man from the south was captivated by the busy promenade, and from the north by the busy neighbors opposite. Due to his growing hunger, Frank decided to visit the nearest store.

As expected, he was greeted by dozens of shelves carrying tons of trinkets as he stepped through the revolving door. They were overwhelming, crying out, "Take me," like a promiscuous woman in a pornographic film.

In this hot time, mineral water was the leader. From the entrance he saw a huge bookcase covered with toilet paper.

As he approached the cash register, he wondered what the pretty cashier she would find. According to Frank, the regularity usually seemed to be that the more expensive the store, the more attractive girls could be found, so that their beauty had a positive effect on the amount of cash spent, the injection of which from the wallet was about to fund the account of one of the tycoons. Seeing the lovely cashier serving him, he thought the store must be really expensive.

Kari with a lush hair the color of raging fire attracted the attention of customers of both sexes. Men looked at her with delight, women with envy. A storm of gently undulating curls flowed irregularly over her shoulders. It was the essence of the new line of Hair Force cosmetics, which he admired on the head of Daria, a model charming with a smile in the catalogs scanned in the lines of hairdressing salons that he happened to visit.

When you receive a shopping scratched her hand his fingernail like a razor.

He decided to get a little closer to her thanks to this innocent incident. And see what will come of it.

For now, he was returning home armed with products to fight the lonely evening, i.e. chocolate pancakes and Cornish patties.

***

He decided to eat in front of the TV, starting by paying attention to the game show of spinning the money wheel and guessing passwords. Wheel of Fortune has been spinning him since childhood. However, of course, there had to be advertising ahead of the program.

Taking his first bite of a chocolate pancake, he watched the woman in her work in a corporation.

A girl with a distorted expression sits at her place in an open space at work. Suddenly the girl jumps up from her seat and starts running. At the same time, a mysterious man dressed in black enters the building. The woman falls into the toilet and a man resembling a Terminator enters the open space where a girl was a moment ago. Like the Terminator, he pulls out a gun and starts shooting people. However, the weapon does not shoot its bullets, but it farts louder and louder. People grab their bellies and the mysterious man enters the toilet where the girl is and opens another door until he reaches her cabin. He forcefully opens the door and fires a shot that bounces back with an even louder fart and hits the attacker who spills across the bathroom floor like a T-1000 in a Terminator.

It turns out that the girl is surrounded by a shield with the name of the pills that she took and the slogan: You are not afraid of constipation! Laxator, it will soften any tough guy attacking you!

In this situation, however, it was difficult to have deeper thoughts. He wondered what was going on. Was this world all about shit anymore? Well, dude must have gotten stiff from that advertised cement, Frank thought as he relished the dish.

Frank, pensive in the starting round, didn't remember much other than the legs of the woman who co-host the show. I guess that was the reason why people there lost their minds and invented unheard of words. Because who would be able not to lose her mind in such circumstances? Ultimately, the finalist was placed in the "Book Title" category. He even chose letters neatly, but time has passed and nothing of it this time. And the password was simple - Bloody City. Who hasn't read this book ?! After all, everyone knew her. - He mocked in his mind.

As usual at times like this, Frank wondered whether to keep watching the show. What kind of psycho chooses these slogans? Some writer's book who must have used more electricity to write it than he made selling it, he thought.

- Something like that with the final slogan?

Funny, he argued with the silent TV. Looking at the woman co-host of the game show, hugging the losing finalist, he thought. - I would like to celebrate the loss in her arms there.

***

After the TV excitement, he started tracking down a charming and threatening female cashier on the Internet. The best way to achieve the goal was to place an advertisement on a social network.
He did not have to wait long - in one of the comments there were indications of the intriguing owner of his lusty thoughts.
He found her profile without much difficulty, but the lack of response from the girl both irritated and stimulated his creativity. So much so that he decided to send a letter to the address of the store

where he met her. It was enough to visit the post office opposite the store where she worked.
He put together a neat text apologizing for a scratched hand while shopping, and went to sleep.

***

On the morning of the next day, he went to post a message. The post office usually sent letters accepted by 2 p.m. on the same day. In this case, it not only shipped, but also delivered.
The result was an evening message from the lovely cashier.

Hello, stranger predatory customer, thank you for your concern, with my hand okay, I'll get out of this :)

Feeling a pleasant shiver spread through his body, Frank wanted to speed up the lazy time to see her again.

***

He visited the store the next day. He looked for Kari in the maze of alleys until he noticed her moving nimbly towards the cash register.
The shapes of the woman seduced the man's fantasy, swaying to the rhythm of her footsteps.
Her hair, gleaming in the early summer sun through the large shop windows, fell over her shoulders like a waterfall in which Frank wanted to sink right now.
The delicate but expressive beauty of the woman drove his senses crazy.

He felt strangely intimidated, like a teenager fighting for the first time for a girl's favor. He asked himself how to continue this relationship. He wondered if she would want to give some lunatic who sent letters a chance to meet her. Because who is doing it nowadays? Only a madman ...

Now it was necessary to follow the blow without wondering what it was like, how to do first and then think. Life will show what happens next. So, without making a more detailed plan, he went with some completely unnecessarily purchased item to the cash register. He wanted to test the reaction, look at those warm lips that promised hot kisses. He wanted to offer her pleasure in his thoughts. To drown in the phenomenal nature of those pistachio rosette eyes, in this fiery gaze.

Last in line, and finally the only one, he wondered how he could have fallen so quickly into a woman. After all, such feelings were alien to him.

Finally, he reached the place of execution, or the cash register, realizing that he had invented nothing that would draw her attention even more. However, the perversity was on his side.

- Are you buying it or are you going to steal it? She asked, disarming him with a smile.

- I'd like to steal your heart! He replied, surprising himself.

- What do you need my heart for?

- I've always dreamed of such a model.

- What would you do with him? She snapped, mentally describing Frank as a plaything.

"This and that, all good things," he defended himself. "Sorry for the hand," he added, backing up a bit to reality.

"Nothing like that happened, an occupational hazard," she joked. - You really can get attention, man.

"Oh, not like you," he replied, making her smile even more radiant.

After a while, the following words were often heard from the cashier's lips:

- Can I owe a coin?

Frank regarded her slyly. Eureka! It struck him.

- Then maybe I will look more carefully - she added after a moment.

- No need, you have my details here, you can bring the coin by the way - he said, giving the address.

- It's not far - Kari said goodbye to a man giving hope tone.

Repeatedly replaying the meeting in his mind, he

could not concentrate on anything else but her.

2. Singles playing in pairs

In the evening, Frank decided to go out somewhere to explore the city.

He was in the bathroom when he heard a knock on the front door. Wanting to get things done quickly, he jumped out, opened and froze at the sight of Kari standing with a coin. View partly naked Frank fell to her liking. She reluctantly allowed him to get dressed.

They went together to explore the area. They walked along the romantically illuminated by lanterns park alleys. They got to know each other until an innocent walk took the couple to a pool club.

Frank led Kari to the table, handed her the stick, and set the balls out.

She looked phenomenal in a dress covering her thighs just below the garters and in the glow of a pool lamp hanging loosely and illuminating the field of play.

The dull glow of the wall sconces showed a soft couch against the wall and a table in the game room that the couple was just occupying.

They looked at each other with eyes eager for the game played for centuries between the two genders. The nakedness of Kari's shoulders combined with the depth of the neckline revealed amazing views with every tilt in the posture typical of a game of billiards. Asking for a few tips, the girl had no idea where this game would lead her.

Frank was happy to get down to work.

He took Kari's delicate hand and placed it on the pleasant-to-touch gown covering the table. He gently parted her fingers, arranged the cue so that the cue could glide over them as well as possible, finally giving it a decisive thrust. Caressing the girl's hand, he noticed how much she enjoyed this lesson. He stood back and slipped the stick into his other hand. Kari grabbed him with a firm grip. They had less and less control over their emotions.

A beautiful woman in the hands of a man, doing whatever he told her to do - such submission was also attractive to her. Uncertainty about what the man would do to her body in a moment, pretending to play, warmed all her senses.

The time has come to put your whole body in the correct posture. Frank started with the legs. One had to stand upright, with no knee bending. He took care of it by stroking her from foot to garter. It was difficult for the girl to obey his orders, as she wanted to lie down on the floor and go crazy with him. However, she bravely kept herself straight.

By touching a tender spot under the knee of the other leg, it caused a slight deflection necessary to maintain proper posture. With each centimeter of exploring the wonderful shapes of her legs, the man's body grew hotter. Pulling his face away from the girl's hips, he leaned over the table. He had Kari's neck within reach of his lips. In this way, he induced her to stretch properly, which was when she could no longer escape from his mouth. He played with her lush hairstyle until their bodies pressed tightly against each other, sensing mutual desire.

Kari's bust resisted the efforts of her male teacher, blocking the simple movement of the stick rubbing too insistently against her breasts. Frank's hands did everything to improve the situation, but the effect was most noticeable in the man's pants. The girl felt more than just the hardness of the stick in her hands. She turned quickly. She gave Frank a sticky look.

They already knew that they would not wait any longer. It had to happen here and now.

The mouth tightened by itself with the force of the railroad carriages to form a unity. Hands with the unpredictability of Brownian motion began to wander over the bodies as if trying to hold them all at once. They both caressed more and more every nook and cranny they managed to reach in the clash of the red-hot bodies.

Frank gripped the girl's hips tighter, propping her up so that she could sit comfortably on the rim of the pool table. She replied quickly, spreading her legs and wrapping them tightly around him. She anchored her heels to the male buttocks taut with excitement.

Grabbing her hair, he tilted her head back. He sank his lips into the delicacy of his neck like an excited vampire. The exciting movements of the woman's hips and the alternating tighter and lighter grip of Kari's strong thighs drove him mad. He wanted so much to be in her already! His lips continued to walk up her neck. Every now and then, a tongue exploring the area from one ear to the other joined them, making Kari erotic trance, sighing, scratching, kissing and caressing. Her hands raged over Frank's body, causing successive waves of shivers that spread out in all directions.

Centimeter by centimeter kissing the hot body of the girl, he reached her shoulders. With his mouth, he pushed the straps of her dress off her shoulders, and it slid gracefully down her smooth, shiny sex body to her hips. Frank moved along with the dress on the woman's body, and then deprived the girl of her panties in a similar way. His eyes saw a lovely sight, obscured by a sexy dress still present at the waist.

Feeling the warmth of the girl's thighs on his cheeks, he kissed their delicate inner side. He was getting closer and closer to the delightful, more and more wet femininity. Arriving at his destination like a summit climber, he gave a gentle kiss. He made her sigh deeper and louder. Tucking her thighs around his head beneath the dress, she made his fly burst open with an unmanageable tension.

Suddenly she released her grip, and instead of her thighs he felt hands on his face. Her hands were pulling his head a little higher. Frank kissed the girl's belly tenderly. It reached the navel.

He dealt with him similarly to her sweet triangle below. First he kissed exactly around, then penetrated with the tip of his tongue inward.

From the navel, his lips traveled to the border of the bra. He reached for the unintentionally yielding clasp. Wrapping his arms around the girl, he gripped the bra with both hands. His muscles tightened, which stimulated the girl even more. Like the sound of a bra ripping that Frank had tossed far away.

The eyes of the man, fired with desire, saw a wonderful sight of firm, swaying breasts. As they exchanged fiery glances, Karii and Frank understood each other without words.

Instantly he grabbed the protruding nipple with his mouth. He sucked with delight. He caressed the other nipple with his fingers. He squeezed both breasts with his strong hands at the same time. He kissed Kari's entire breasts, helping himself with his tongue, the tip of which made the woman ecstatic. He was touching the hard tops of the nipples, grasping them whole after a while. It wrapped itself on them like a pancake with a nipple filling.

- Fuck me at last…! She whispered, sliding off the table.

"I want you," it rained from both lips.

She threw off the remnants of her clothes. Unbuttoning the man's fly, she deftly released his penis outside.

He jumped out like crazy. Freed from his pants, he fell directly captive to Kari's mouth. She greeted him with a kiss, which deftly exposed his shining head. She gripped the penis in one hand, caressing tenderly. She grabbed the scrotum with

her other hand, playing with the man's testicles
more and more boldly.

She squeezed and kissed the penis from root to
tip, deftly wrapping her tongue around it. She
licked like a mad snake until she finally sucked
with such ferocity that Frank felt as if his penis
had reached her vagina through her throat.

Barely holding back the shot, he pushed his penis
into kari's mouth as if it were in her vagina.

Feeling very close to an eruption, he grabbed her
tousled hair.

He pulled her lips away from the sucked, erect
penis, sprinkled with the first drops of sperm
coming out.

She lay down on the sofa in the shaded corner of
the billiard room. Spreading her legs, she invited
him to her place. It immediately reached her wet
cavity. He licked the rim with the tip of his

tongue, not forgetting to pay special attention to the clitoris. He penetrated the vagina deeply, penetrating the whirling tongue more and more. He kissed a hot, wet vagina like a mouth. Hot, passionate and passionate. His hands gripped her ass. He caressed the stomach and any place he could reach.

Kari held him tightly with her thighs. At times she let go. She screamed and kicked with delight in all directions like a raging doe.

She seduced the man with all her might, her touch across Frank's body as if she wanted to squeeze all of him inside a vagina burning with desire. Ecstatic convulsions rocked her body. She drifted off for a moment, laying down on top of him. She calmed down a bit, but the sight of the powerful erection did not allow for a longer rest. She grabbed his penis.

She picked up her billiard teacher from the sofa and led him to the table. She caressed with one hand and grabbed his ass with the other.

She whispered, biting his ear:

- This is a touchdown to the shot ...

She pulled the man away. She grabbed his steel buttock predatorily. She froze and moved Frank forward. She played the ball on the table with his erect penis. The ball hit another one that bounced off the opposite cushion. The pool ball started coming back.

Kari stopped the ball between her breasts, leaning alluringly over the table.

He did not stand it. He grabbed her shapely bottom, slipped all his toned manhood into it. Sighing, he bit her ear. He put the stick lying on the table under Kari's stomach. He tried to bring the game to an end. He moved the stick, caressed the tender places between his breasts. He rested the stick on her hand, which clawed at the cloth on the pool table.

He made successive thrusts. He froze in motion with each one, and after a while he penetrated the girl leaning over the table harder and faster. Playing the ball, he slipped deep into her fiery vagina. He caressed the belly. He played the game precisely on and off the table with the stick and the member. He drove the girl crazy with delight to madness.

Lusty sighs caressed her ears. They kindled the heat that spread between the breasts in all directions. He caressed the womb. The thrill of pleasure was connected on the woman's back with the man's body, which provided her with unimaginable sensations.

A caressing slap against the plump buttock was a

sign to move in the right direction. She teased, wanting more of them, listening to the erotic melodies flowing from the loudspeaker in the pool room where they were.

The last move of the stick ... The last black ball driven into the pocket ... The last moves in the pocket of Kari ...

And their first room-filling orgasm together. Both lost in each other, stretched out in ecstasy, they fell down on the table, nibbling, caressing and kissing in the madness of the moment.

They spent their last moments in the Room of Exultations intertwined, watching the table from the sofa - the place of foreplay and subsequent sharp fulfillment without brakes.

A light flashed, signifying that the game time was up in a few minutes.

After settling down, they walked over to the bar.

Kari's incomplete outfit was a memento of a wonderful time. The lack of a bra and stockings teased Frank's fantasy.

***

Before leaving the club, he suggested one more game, this time a bar game, i.e. drinking alcohol by the gram. It consisted in choosing drinks placed on the scale in a bar. They had to be drunk in turns, in small sips. The winner was the one who hit a certain weight perfectly. Alternatively, the one who drank too much, even by a gram, was the loser. The loser was to fulfill the winner's wish.

And so Kari started the challenge to the sounds of music. After her sip, there was still a lot to drink. Distracted by the girl's trailing gaze, Frank took a deep sip, drawing him closer to victory.

However, the difficult task Kari did brilliantly, just soaking her mouth in her Bellini. She won the struggle with the drink perfectly. Then her lips glittered even brighter, encouraging a peach kiss. A thrill of uncertainty ran through Frank's body, he wondered what the girl would come up with as a wish.

***

After leaving the club, they felt the evening heat radiating from the street. Along it, there were rows of polytechnic buildings and dormitories on the other side.

They walked in the middle of the tram rails, entwined with each other. Nobody or anything existed until they heard a distinctive sound behind their backs.

It is difficult to judge which was louder: the bell or the scolding cries of the tram driver.

But they didn't bother with it, as they hurried across the last few meters. They got a tram at the stop. Standing in the rear of the almost empty wagon, joined in a tender embrace, they rejoiced at each other.

They found the romanticism of the moment in tenement houses, crossroads and illuminated lamps running backwards. There was something else in the air besides the smell of trees and mowed grass.

Not noticing that they were alone in the tram, they drove along a tree-lined alley straight to the tram terminus.

A dead door trapped them inside. The driver left somewhere in the direction he knew only.

"I have a wish," Kari said suddenly.

- Listen?

"Don't listen, just take it out now," she said in an imperative, warm tone.

The screeching of the trouser zipper confirmed her wish. Frank slid his penis out for her, waved it cheerfully.

"Sweet," she said, stroking her hand over the stately penis. - You quickly raise the barrier. Would you like to go all the way? She asked playfully, approaching the swollen penis, encouraging both of them to take another dose of pleasure.

The man was very eager. Unable to say anything, he gave himself to the unexpected caress, just as he stood.

The clever hands of the girl quickly stretched the phallus pulsating with desire. As she did so, she kept staring into Frank's burning eyes. She watched him drift away as she ran her fingers over him. She caressed once more gently, then harder again. She grabbed with her hands revealing and covering the acorn. She squeezed evenly inch by inch. At the same time she was playing with the scrotum still hidden in his pants. He was flexing really hard for her, thirsty for a shot.

She made him grab the railing behind his back and forbade any touching of her body. Pulling the dress up, it irritated the man's senses. She wrapped her legs around Frank's hips with her bent knee, tightly pressing the buttocks with her calf, so that his erect penis rubbed against her thigh hidden under a carelessly lowered dress. He tapped his penis at her femininity covered in skimpy panties. He was reaching up to her buttocks with his cock, twisting like a grass snake in the hay.

She gripped the advancing penis harder. She was massaging a different place with it every now and then. She slipped it on as and where she wanted. With the delight she gave him, Frank saw the stars. At the same time, chills seized his body. He barely stayed on his feet when she for a moment slipped his penis thirsty for penetration into her panties. She rocked her bottom neatly. She gave him hope, but hadn't let him in yet, toying with his male lust.

She was squeezing the ass of the blue-eyed "Thor" in the iron vice of her wonderfully muscled leg, as if she wanted to squeeze it all over, like paste out of a tube, through his hard penis pumped with her caresses. She reached the heights of ecstasy with him, but would not let him shoot.

She said firmly:

- You'll cum if I let you.

It gave him unbelievable excitement.

She rubbed and tormented a large penis. She kissed the man's torso, reaching his mouth across his neck. The more passionately he kissed her lips, the closer he was to fulfillment, and she controlled the intensity of his caresses.

The blush on her face and the pleasant warmth of a moist, delightful female triangle massaged insistently with a penis, convinced him of the pleasure she took from the caress she gave.

He begged for fulfillment, whispering between kisses in his ear:

- Do this to me, let ... Kariii ...!

"Try your best," she said, then turned away. She took her lover's hand off the railing and tucked it into her panties.

- Caress me! She moaned, biting Frank's ear.

- You are wonderful! He said excitedly, slipping his finger into her slit, squeezing it like a juicy tangerine.

- Now do it! She exclaimed, digging her fingers into the excited male ass.

She was tugging at her buttock. With her other hand she tugged the taut phallus, rubbing it mercilessly back and forth until it fired.

He flooded everything around with freshly squeezed semen like a fire hose with water.

- Oh, Kari.

He cuddled her tenderly. She was so shaky, smelling wonderful. Bathed in the night light of lamps peering between the trees into the windows of a tram car.

The sleepy atmosphere was interrupted by the

appearance of the driver, finally checking the wagons.

The couple ended a relatively successful evening at Kari's door, saying goodbye with a tender kiss, as it was not appropriate for a woman to invite a man inside at the first meeting.

***

The next morning, Frank was due to report to his new job. More for entertainment than by duress. The years spent in the special services became an interesting memory.

Frank did not know how he did it, that he survived in this formation for so long, despite his difficult character, which was not broken by any procedures, fossilized regulations or often Spartan living conditions.

Friends looked at him with a mixture of amusement, contempt and surprise as he announced that he was going to Singles Town, to become an ordinary bodyguard.

For work in which patience was more important than rich experience. And the ability to endure humiliation by everyone around you. A security guard for buildings, parking lot or a supermarket is, in the opinion of many, no one. Someone to humiliate. But that was exactly what he needed - a change.

He locked his medals in a drawer, along with papers documenting the vast majority of his brilliant career. To become a serial nobody, with no past and no future, but with an expressive present.

The job of patrolling the darkest corners of the city was, in his opinion, ideal to internally make your life a little more meaningful.

For now, he had arrived in the hall by six in the morning, where security had directed him to another part of the building, where he would wait for someone to lead him to yet another new assignment.

It was six, then ten past six, then twenty, and he was about to leave when just before seven a weary guard appeared.

However, they did not forget about him. Overall, he was starting to like the place because the situation was a harbinger of a general mess. And in fact, nobody cared. In the general confusion, he finally made it to the spot. There the belly-headed mustache man greeted him with an apology for forgetting. All in all, Frank didn't mind and found it a plus. However, he did not betray his joy. Then he was given his new position without delay.

- Please sit down. The coach said.

Following the mustache's command, he looked around the room with a bad feeling. Watching the intensity of the work, he fell into the trap of yawning. The upside was the absolute lack of mobbing. It was just a genius of idleness filling the room.

- Welcome to the monitoring.

- How is it "on monitoring"? He was indignant.

- In your application you indicated ...

- Everything except monitoring! He pouted, not letting the belly man finish.

"Shit, indeed," the man said, biting his mustache. Eventually he revealed some emotions.

- Well, from tomorrow there will be a car and the rest of the equipment, but today here - he added soothingly.

The belly man in a few jumps found himself in the office, making a fuss.

And so Frank's first day at work was spent mainly watching single women rushing to different parts of the city. The women looked seductive, smiled and furious.

***

This time it was going to be a movie night. Kari appeared in Frank's apartment even prettier than the day before. With flowing, curly hair that covers her shoulders. A modest blouse and a loose skirt of a reasonable length added to the charm she exuded with every movement.

They held their senses with all their might lest the affectionate greeting would end up like the last meeting at the pool table.

The first film in the repertoire of the couple was
The Color of Money. While they survived its
projection calmly, when the Stripteaser appeared
on the screen, the senses made themselves felt.
At one point, Frank felt something beautiful on
his cheek. Kari's foot.
He immediately caught her in the mouth. Kissing
tenderly, he looked into the girl's wonderful,
seductive eyes. She watched his reaction. He
kissed the toes one by one. The film has become
just a background shimmering on Kari's shining
body.
After the toes it was time for the rest of the foot,
the back and looking for tickles underneath.
Moving to the ankle, he peered rudely higher.
With his fiery gaze he made the girl shiver. Chills
ran more and more under the playfully upturned
skirt. Sensitive areas hidden under the thongs

were burning.

The temperature of desire was not cooled by the milk-white sofa they were on. The bed made the sound of frozen snow crackling under the foot of a walker in the freezing cold of a moonlit night. With his hands, Frank was ahead of kissing lips. He wandered along the leg, higher and higher. He stroked the calf thoroughly, reached the knee. Mina Kari said it all. The bitten lips showed how much pleasure he gave her. Enjoying his lips on the softer part of his thigh, he kissed higher and higher, excited by the last straight to the goal. She spread her legs bent at the knees. The skirt ran down the velvet of her thighs to her hips with the lightness of a mountain stream caressing the rock. She did not let the man get higher. She put the other, still un-kissed foot over Frank's mouth. She forced him to start his caressing work anew, like Sisyphus. She pushed him a little to the other side of the bed. She relished the sight of the thirsty man's beauty conquering her again.

It slowly annexed areas of the other leg. Centimeter by centimeter. He kissed and massaged thoroughly. He stroked and kneaded tenderly. He did it with increasing passion, feeling the girl's kissed foot slide over his bare torso. Lower and lower. She was heading towards his sensitive places.

Suddenly he felt that the other foot was already there. She was rubbing Frank's crotch over his pants. His manhood grew tougher. Coming out of the bend just behind the girl's knee, he saw a woman's gesture of invitation under her skirt.

He was already gliding. He stroked her thigh with his face. He tugged his foot raging in his pants, bringing his penis upright.

Until suddenly the sound of the phone ringing ruined everything.

Kari, not wanting to spoil the fun, ignored the sounds coming from the next room, but the caller's insistence did not give her peace. She pulled away from Frank's mouth. She picked up an intrusive call. The caller clearly wanted sex from her.

Well, Singles City, there's no relationship here, Frank thought, disgusted with the fact that Kari wasn't just his.

She turned on the speakerphone so that you could clearly hear the conversation. The caller was clearly playing with himself. He tried to get her to do the same. She wanted to end this conversation, but Frank stopped her. At the same time, he released the taut penis from his pants. He slipped it into her hand. Just like the man on the phone wanted it.

She gave Frank a strange look, but took up the challenge. They began to do realistically what her lover wanted to do virtually on the phone.

They started massaging the penis. They listened to the story of a man how tough he is and how he wants to fuck her now.

Frank also had a swollen penis, so she got down to business. She bared the acorn with her tongue. She teased the tip tenderly. Already at this point, the nature wanted to explode. She grabbed it with both hands. She started massage more and more. She sucked harder and deeper, as she absorbed the hard to the limit of the endurance of the body. Kari gave another caress to the swollen penis. She grabbed it, lovingly playing with its shape. She twisted it like no other woman had ever done before. She started sucking at the same time, caressing with tonsils. She scratched deeper and deeper around the testicles. Kari drove him to such a state that Frank was losing touch with reality.

- Why don't you say anything? Asked an excited voice from the phone.

"Because I was sucking on a hard, excited cock," she replied, quickly sliding down from Frank's swollen penis, choking on air as she did so. She did it so suddenly he almost fired off the suddenness of her movement.

"Now get on me and ride me," a voice said from the phone.

"You wouldn't last long," she replied, savoring the hardness of the male attribute in her vagina.

The sofa groaned. Frank felt Kari devouring his magnificent penis with his delicate pussy. She dominated him with more and more intense movements of her hips. Washing in the washing machine does not live up to what she gave his penis. She moved her ass in all directions.

The man in subjection writhed under her. His hands caressed her bouncing breasts and belly. He grabbed the pretty, prominent bum she was now working so hard at for their joint orgasm. Scratching the man's torso, she fell on him. She hugged him and bit him on the neck. She covered his face with her hair.

The telephone companion was now completely on fire. He begged Kari for fulfillment. Frank was completely mesmerized by the hopping of her lovely breasts, topped with firmly protruding nipples.

The girl let out a delightful groan. She stuck her nails into her lover's torso. She leaned over to him, throwing in her lush haircut. She hugged it

with breathtaking strength and gave it a brutal
kiss. She tightened even more the murderous grip
of her ass on her battered penis.

- I want to cum on you now! A voice called on the
phone.

- Squirt. - She sighed.

She slid down onto the bed slowly, completely
ignoring the fact that Frank didn't want to get out
of her right now.

They clasped their hands together, playing with
their swollen penis. The vigorous massage
brought them closer to the eruption. With a blurry
glance, she admired how the huge cock strained
in front of her, ready to fire.

The voice in the earpiece released its tension first.
Moments later, Kari led Frank's member to an
eruption with a few movements. Her face was
flooded with a torrent of hot, sticky semen. The

power of the ejaculation made her have them everywhere. In the hair, forehead and eyelids. Her smiling lips were drowned in the sticky juice that also reached her breasts and stomach.

Frank kissed her tenderly. Both, with a taste for what they had experienced, sat naked. Huddled together. Both dirty with their last experience.

***

Eventually they went to shower to refresh their bodies and minds.

Frank watched with delight as the first drops wet Kari's wavy hair, then ran down her face, then wrapped around her shoulders and ran a trickle between her breasts. Drops washed the navel and went between the legs. A trickle ran down Kari's thighs and calves to her feet.

Watching the water pranks on Kari's body, Frank felt her hands slide into his hair with the shampoo, soaping it thoroughly. The wonderful relaxation fueled by the multitude of kisses and the touch of prominent breasts on his naked body stimulated all the senses. Another lusty feeling engulfing him completely. He took incredible joy, even just soaping Kari's back. Centimeter by centimeter, they were lost in the foam, from the shoulder blades to the loins, caressed along with the butt in circular movements. Back through the spine he provided the girl with lazy pleasure. He made sure that none of the circles were left out. He was getting her fissure between her buttocks. He caressed it with his fingers along with the stream of water.

Kari returned the caresses until she felt that something is standing between them. Then she chased the man out of the cabin to torment him with a phenomenal view of her naked body through the glass. She pressed her breasts against the glass wall. He immediately clung to the other side excitedly. He kissed her through the glass. Suddenly she gently opened the door.

"Slip it in here," she said, reaching out to her tense cock.

She took him deeply until he felt the doorframe. She turned and arched her butt. She grabbed the penis. She tightened her legs tightly, grasping the penis with her thighs. Now he could feel her every move as she washed her body. She caressed her breasts. She moved her bum in accordance with their rhythm.

Reaching the vagina, she lathered a hard penis. He tensed in a merciless grip between her thighs. She was careful that it did not fire too quickly.

She asked for a towel.

The man obeyed immediately. He slipped it into the cabin on a stretched penis. The girl put a towel on herself and tied it above her breast. Frank pulled her out quickly. He ordered her to lean against the wall. He proceeded to the search like a policeman.

- Put your legs wide to the sides! He ordered firmly. She obediently obeyed. "More," he repeated.

However, it was still not wide enough.

He pulled up the towel. He discovered the girl's ass. He punished her on both buttocks. He slipped the hard attribute of power between her thighs and spread Kari's legs wide. He used his penis like a police baton.

The girl felt an exciting respect for the hardness of the penis pressing against her, which made her obey. She stood as ordered, her hands resting on the wall. He ripped the towel off Kari. He was wiping the girl's insane body hard. He was carrying out a personal inspection. He clung to her tightly. He gripped the firm breasts tenderly in his hands and wiped the water off them in a circular motion. He was scrubbing his back with his bare chest.

The swollen member rubbed the buttocks with the grace of a bow dancing on the strings, irritating sensitive places with virtuosity. He kissed the wet hair flowing down her neck. He caressed both ears tenderly. Rapid breathing in Kari's undulating chest revealed her emotions bursting through her nipples.

The towel flew into the air. The man entered her. He was delving into control. The girl sighed delightfully.

He pushed slowly. The spanking shook Kari's sexy ass. The girl shook her ass steadily, providing both of them with strong sensations. He caressed every nook and cranny of the girl's body with his hands. He kissed tenderly. He penetrated it slowly, harder and deeper. Grabbing sensitive places, he caressed them. He worked deeply in a woman more and more decisively.

She was trembling, sighing harder and harder.

"Oh yeah, yeah," she cheered. "Take me harder, don't stop," she pleaded.

He did not stop. He penetrated her mercilessly, until her body spasms.

Scratching the grout between the bathroom tiles with her fingernails, she collapsed into Frank's arms.

He did not let her rest long.

"We're going to bed," he ordered.

She carried out the command. She walked towards the bedroom, guided by the man's strained body. He did not leave her damp vagina for a moment. Each step contained their bodies in trembling union.

He tossed her on the soft bed. She bit her lip. She looked at the shiny member. She waited for what he would do next.

The penis swayed over her face like a protruding pendulum. He irritated the senses, he teased. Frank didn't let the girl get hold of his penis. He wiped her cheeks with it. He slipped it into his hair. It tickled the neck. He was walking blindly. Finally he pressed against his face, covering his eyes.

She studied the huge, hard, throbbing penis. She tickled him with her lashes, her whole body ready to be owned again. She caught him in the mouth as he stood. She sucked with all her might. She was scratching Frank's tense buttocks. She wanted to tear them apart. She pressed harder. She wanted it to be in her mouth stronger and deeper.

At the same time, the man used his tongue to reach the depths of the sweet, juicy womb of Kari. Oral caresses of the vagina encouraged the girl to touch her hard penis more courageously. She licked it madly along its entire length. She did not forget about the testicles. She consumed him. It led to the brink of endurance.

Cheating the incoming ejaculation, the man raised his hips. He ripped the penis out of the mouth of the red-haired nymph, but she kept the man in check, clenching her legs around his neck. She grasped the taut penis with her lips while it was still in the air. Frank collapsed onto the bed with a pleasant expression on his face, which she quickly took advantage of, sitting on his face.

He pressed his lips to the girl's ass. He kissed her buttocks. He stuck his tongue into the caressing inside of the vagina, which had been worked out a moment earlier by his penis, which she had reached again with her mouth. She abused mercilessly. She was an absolute champion in this.

He could just feel her pliable tongue inside his penis.

Excited by the raging tongue in her vagina, she swallowed the vigorously taut manhood with her lips to the very testicles. She caressed like crazy.

"I'll give you an orgasm now," she sighed.

- Nothing of that. I will decide about it.

He rose behind her back. His arms grabbed her breasts. After a while he was entering her from

behind, kneeling on the bed. He pushed his hard
club into the tight cavern. She was rolling the
sheet in clenched handfuls as it pressed hard.
With the last of his strength he overcame the
pressure of sperm ready to shoot. He tried to give
his partner as much pleasure as possible.
He stepped out of her interior for a moment. He
turned the passive and distracted Kari on her
back. Then he slipped imperiously even more
forcefully into her shivering body.
- I want to see your face to the end. - Frank said.
- Watch and fuck me hard! She gasped as she
waited for the sticky shower.
They twine their fingers together to form unity.
The man stretched Kari's hands above her head.
He kissed the face, neck and hair. He kissed
everywhere, not letting her defend herself. He
was going in faster and harder. He penetrated

deeply into the most hidden nooks and crannies.
He bit his ear brutally. It was like a jackhammer,
crushing the remains of her vaginal resistance.
The bed moved with them, squeaking and
creaking to the rhythm of their bodies. Only
Kari's screams were louder. The girl's body
stretched.
Frank's penis exploded. He flooded her femininity
with a huge amount of freshly pressed sperm.
The girl's skin glistened intensely. Its healthy
color shimmered in the light of the moon peeking
through the curtains not fully closed.
A red dot appeared on Frank's neck and followed
his back. It went over the buttocks. She visited
the nooks and crannies of Kari.

What lovebirds in love. I'll cut their feathers,
thought the figure stroking the naked bodies of

the couple with a laser dot.

Not noticing anything, exhausted, they hugged each other. Taking advantage of the fact that his penis was losing toughness very slowly, Frank was still in Kari. He was still bathing in the lake of pleasure. He slowly remembered what it was like to hug someone goodnight. Someone with whom he wants to wake up the next day.

***

- You have! The man placed his revolver in front of the kneeling Frank. With the barrel towards him. - You know how it goes on, should I explain the rules to you?
"I know," Frank replied, taking the revolver with one empty chamber in the barrel in his hand. He

put it against his temple.

  He looked into the lifeless eyes of the woman with a gun to his head. He knew it was over, because the psychopathic stranger wasn't joking. He gritted his teeth, hoping to find a full chamber. Let the cartridge take away his and his empty life. "The rules of Russian roulette are a little different," Frank said.

"In my version, there is always someone killed," the stranger grumbled.

The situation was as follows: if Frank hits the cartridge chamber, he will commit suicide and Kari will be saved. If he finds an empty one, then the stranger will pull the trigger, taking the girl's life.

- Faster because I'll pull the trigger without a game and you'll have this redhead on your conscience.

Frank considered several possibilities, but yielded to the thug's will. He pulled the trigger ...

And nothing.

Kari!

There was a bang and ...

The morning greeted Frank with a lonely wake-up call in bed. Murmurs from the kitchen reached his ears. Sleepy, he jumped up to check the source of the suspicious sounds. He looked into the room. Kari stopped exercising her crunches to ask with a captivating smile:

- Did you dream about something interesting?

"No, nothing interesting, some kind of nightmare," he replied, wiping the cold sweat from his brow.

"So dreaming about me is a nightmare?" She mocked him. "You're lucky you screamed my name in your sleep or you would have just seen a nightmare." She acted irritated, frowning.

She amused him with her sweet face. He approached the girl, giving her a captivating smile.

- You, my sweet tease. He kissed her, straightening the lines on her forehead. He was delighted to see Kari in a short T-shirt and no underwear.

Seeing the impression she made on him, she added a trailing look to her smile as she resumed her exercises.

He stood frozen to the beauty of her body. Nature quickly began to do its job. He came out of the kitchen but his penis began to rise. Losing to lust, the man returned.

The penis entered the kitchen first, then Frank. Kari petrified seeing what she had done, and her eyes lit up.

Grasping the girl's hands, he quickly picked her up from the floor and sat her on a cupboard. Without any questions, he started kissing her lovely, moist, full lips. The hands themselves found the right places.

Her legs tightened on his loins. She was attracted to herself. Teamed up, they began to greet the morning. They made a mess on the cupboard. The rays of the morning sun caressed their entwined bodies. They both wanted to do it fast and hard.

They ignited each other when they saw the sparks in their partner's eyes. They bit their necks like predators in the hunt. He loved to feel her tremble under the pressure of his tongue.

He operated it from her shoulder to her ear. He licked them, kissed them, and slid gently inward, which made her press Frank tighter against her with the iron grip of her strong legs.

She was scratching the man's back hard. She slipped her hand between her legs. She caught a hard penis squeezing between her thighs. He wandered over her warm, throbbing womb. Resting her knees against her stomach, she did not allow for a close-up. She rubbed a penis inside her full thighs. She teased herself by attracting and pushing away her partner. He massaged the girl's legs with his penis, from the feet to the gate of delightful femininity, still unable to penetrate inside, because she hid it from him when he was too close.

He was up between Kari's lap. He began to stimulate the tender spot under one of her knees with his penis. She tightened them tighter on him. She wrapped it up so that it felt like a vagina.

Frank moved him as if he were actually inside. She watched the man's ass tighten with every movement. The awareness of the hard penis under the knee had a strong influence on the woman's senses attacked by chills.

He caressed her thighs, knees and calves. Eventually he laced the fingers of his hand with the toes of her foot. He gripped his hair tightly with his other hand. He bit her neck, then released her. Hair flew in all directions.

He caressed the cheeks, neck, breasts, hardening nipples. He moved his hand towards the stomach. He paid attention to the navel. It reached her juicy vagina. He was touching his finger deeper and deeper inside. He did all this to the rhythm of the penis working under Kari's knee, he provided his partner with impressions. The blushes painted her face better than any makeup.

He was crushing her juicy cunt. He watched the girl close her eyes. She demanded fulfillment, with her other leg caressing the man's loins and buttocks. She slid her foot between them. It irritated the senses of the man, so he penetrated her even more intensely.

When she released her grip, his mouth fell to the womb. He went crazy with circular movements. He put his tongue as deeply as he could. He listened to the expressive sounds made by Kari. He quickly pulled her to the floor.

She grabbed the faucet and anchored herself on the sink. A hard member entered her from behind. He massaged the vagina briskly. Right away, straightforward, without questions or thinking. He penetrated the wet femininity mercilessly.

They were demolishing the sink squeaking beneath them. Frank grabbed the girl by the knee, raised it higher to better get into the girl. He grabbed her bouncing breasts. He was biting her neck. He satisfied the woman with strong and quick movements of the steel penis.

He made Kari scream out in obscene words what she had just felt.

He did not give the heated vagina a moment of respite. He pushed her in all directions until he felt that Kari was about to come to orgasm.

At this point, he pulled it out. He pulled the girl towards him and began to search for her mouth with his penis.

She turned, colliding the delicacy of her lips with the brutal hardness of the taut phallus. Her sweet lips sucked him mercilessly. It drove him to the shot.

She bravely took a heavy ejaculation, bringing out a deep sigh from the man.

She saw the silent thanks for fulfillment in his blind eyes and in kisses offered in equally generous numbers.

***

After an exciting morning, it's time to go to the workplace.

There was another training day spent still monitoring. Only the next one was going to be more interesting, as Frank was supposed to go a bit outside the city to undergo intensive training of patrol formations.

For now, he glanced once at the screen, once at Thunderbolt sitting against the far wall, wondering if it was still alive. The surname did not necessarily correspond to his lifestyle. It was amazing how statically he was doing his job. He

made a move maybe every quarter of an hour.
He made himself a cup of tea and ate breakfast,
then went on to complete the routines.

First of all - the list with monitors. The number
one monitor is? He felt and stroked the monitor -
it was indeed. And so are all the rest. Another
card asked if the monitor was operational. The
monitors were all working. It was what got on his
nerves the most. He wondered what it would be
like to indicate that the monitor was gone, but it
was working.

Then - do the cameras work. These procedures
were the reverse of a hair shampoo. Instead of
three in one, it's three out of one. But it wasn't his
business why you had to fill out three pages
instead of one.

It wasn't over yet. It still remained to check the
recorders, the fire cabinet and the CB radio.

Everything was fine and working. Aside from the resolution of some cameras where it was difficult to tell the dog from the cow, it was all fine. Meanwhile, another man came to clean the air conditioning, as Frank understood well.

- What are you doing this for? Everything is dismantled there. It's been down for two years… - said one of Frank's senior colleagues.

- Does not matter. They pay me per point, not for it still working. Still works in the documents. He sprayed the air conditioner and walked away. The attendants then tested the connectivity so Frank had to answer them. A few more security tests, and after about two hours he looked at the cameras intently for the first time. Perfect timing as the manager was approaching. Seeing him in the camera, he quickly put headphones over his ears to tease him.

The manager fell out of the elevator, as nervous as ever. The clap of the door handle was not yet silent, and it was already possible to hear:

- Fraaank! Damn it, take off those headphones!

Frank didn't react at all to the manager's shouting, which made the man even more irritated. He walked over to Frank and slapped him on the back.

- Oh, honorable manager. Frank shuddered. He pretended to notice his supervisor only now. He took one receiver out of his ear and asked, "It's a lovely day today, isn't it, sir?"

"Yours will be worse soon," replied the manager.

- What are you listening to there again? You know you have to listen to me. Headphones are prohibited! There will be a punishment!

- But dear manager ... - Frank objected, with difficulty maintaining the seriousness - you can not stop listening to such a good audiobook ...

He pointed to the headphone cord tucked between the pages of the most paperback version of Bloody City.

Frank waited impatiently for the evening. He was still thinking about Kari.

Finally, Piorun stood up, hitting the door right, which meant the longed-for end of boredom.

***

A beautiful summer evening, caressing the senses with an aromatic breeze, made it lazy, introducing a sleepy mood. At the same time, it stimulated both Kari and Frank in a romantic way to the surrounding world.

Upon entering Kari's apartment, the man was greeted by a warm interior.

The dimmed light added mystery to the delicate scent of the perfume in which the girl was dressed under a skimpy, airy dress.

- You look great and you have a captivating smile.

"Thank you, my romantic," she replied with a perceptible note of distraction.

- Is something wrong? - He asked.

- Why do you think so?

- Maybe I don't know you much, but I have the impression that you are somehow absent.

- Everything's all right. I wonder if we don't lack variety.

- What do you mean?

The girl intrigued him.

- Do you like having fun in a larger group? She asked carefully.

- How big?

"Two by one, two by two, just plain," she replied, as if triangles or other polygons were natural. But they were in Singles Town.

- Now the two of us will have to suffice for you. Me and him, he said, pointing to his pants, and kissed the girl on the lips.

Not allowing the conversation to continue, he led her to a table on which stood a basket full of fruit. Standing behind him, he picked up a juicy orange and began peeling it slowly. He did it with his firm, delightful mouth.

- How sweet your orange is.

Kari quickly took up the challenge, grabbing the tail of a plump banana. At the same time, Frank bit a few particles to release their juice, running the tip of his tongue over each of them, licking the sticky sweetness.

Kari, keeping eye contact, grasped the banana with her teeth. She peeled the skin with slow, long movements. She captured the imagination of a man.

He immediately bit harder at the orange, sucking the juice from the inside of the fruit. With your thirsty lips. Juice ran down his chin.

Seeing the agitation of the man, the girl dealt with her phallic fruit even more passionately. She wrapped her tongue around the banana. She molested with her mouth. She pushed it deep into her mouth, then ejected it smoothly. She licked the tip and bit off with sparks in her eyes. She swallowed, licking her lips. She gave Frank a seductive smile.

He felt the tightness of his pants, especially when Kari, sliding down the shoulder of her dress, exposed her chest. She started rubbing it with a banana. She slipped it between them and squeezed it, biting off another piece.

Noticing that the bulge in Frank's pants had reached a solid shape, she opened his zipper. She let the penis outside. He jumped out taut, ready for action.

She took the tired orange from the man's hand and stuck it on the red-hot penis.

Moving it further, Frank penetrated deeper and deeper into it. Eventually he burst it completely in Kari's hand. He poured the juice over her face, cleavage and the entire girl's dress. She licked the splashed penile juice to the testicles dripping orange nectar.

She got up, all dirty and lovely. She kissed him. It was a wonderfully citrus kiss.

Still holding a banana in her hand, she touched the erected phallus, comparing their size. He took the fruit from her hands and slipped it under her dress. Lifting her airy clothes, he enjoyed the sight of the beautiful womb. He slipped the fruit in affectionately, rubbing Kari's throbbing vagina until she bit her lips.

As the entire pubic mound took on a banana flavor, he took the remnants of the banana into his mouth. He ate with love. He knelt in front of her fruity femininity. Kari lowered her dress, covering the man's head with it. Leaning against the wardrobe, she gave him access to her womb. He kissed the throbbing triangle inch by inch, never missing a bit. He licked her like crazy, made her shudder through her body. She tapped her hands on the closet door. She was sighing louder and louder. Crossing her leg on her lover's neck, she demanded stronger and deeper caresses. He penetrated deeply with his tongue. He kissed her swollen labia. He licked every bulge, crevice and crease. He held her firm ass in his hands. Kari swayed more and more, unable to stand still. She tensed her body, screaming. She tightened on Frank's body. She was eating him with an exploding vagina.

She fell into male arms, not forgetting the protruding organ. She tucked it between her breasts. She moved up and down several times, tightening the firm rim of her breasts around it. He fired a volley of warm, smelling of fulfillment sperm. It flooded her chin, neck, breasts and her crumpled and dirty dress.

They went on like that for a long moment, figuratively and literally sticking together, then went to the bathroom, sincerely willing to take a bath. The girl chose a bathtub, Frank was left with a shower.

They watched each other's naked bodies. At first, the separation was working out quite well, but seeing the girl's body glisten soaked with white foam, Frank's desire to help her in the bath grew in direct proportion to his penis stimulated by the stream of water.

The man walked over and grabbed the girl's leg.

- You didn't even last a quarter of an hour?

- As you can see. Get ready to dive! Pipe first, he said imperiously, mesmerizing her with his swaying penis.

"Nothing of that," she defended herself.

He handed her an excited penis like a diving pipe. He rubbed the girl's cheeks with it. He was getting fuller.

She stopped resisting fun. She felt it in her mouth. She grabbed it and sucked it deeply. She caressed the body with copious foam. It changed Frank's expression in an incredibly attractive way to Kari.

He bent down and put his hand under the water.

He dipped his hand slowly between his breasts. It glided through the belly, penetrated the navel. He headed for her sunken cave.

The hand has reached its target. Unable to go deeper, he froze on the girl in the "69" position. Delighted with the smoothness of his legs, he kissed them thoroughly.

She did not stop sucking the dick for a moment. Frank plunged his head under the water. The air supply in the man's huge lungs allowed him to penetrate the nooks and crannies between the female legs for a long time. He was blowing air bubbles inside. He made a real jacuzzi in her bosom. He did not forget about the gap between the buttocks.

The caress stimulated Kari to play more

intensively with her partner's penis. Bubbles in the vagina led the girl to scream out Frank's name.

He was flooding her mouth with more semen. She looked lovely, bathed in foam and ejaculation. Bestowing a man with her furiously delightful gaze.

***

As he was leaving the bathroom, he heard a knock on the door. He opened it and greeted a neighbor.

- You turn this porn down, you can hear it through the ceiling! - The stranger cried.

- Kari, quieter! Frank shouted towards the bathroom, passing the information.

When she finally took a quiet bath, he examined the apartment. He noticed an infatuation with music. He found extensive karaoke equipment. He immediately came up with an idea how to use it differently than the manufacturer had anticipated.

Hearing the girl leaving the bathroom, he greeted her with the nakedness of his statuesque body. She entered the living room, wearing a transparent petticoat. She beamed at the sight of the naked man holding the guitar with the strings facing him. At the slightest touch, his instrument came to life, depending on the force of tugging and touching it.

Romantic music flowed from the speakers. Kari started dancing to the rhythm alluringly. She made bolder and bolder movements to which Frank's masculinity could not remain indifferent.

The girl grabbed the microphone lying on the cupboard. And after a while there was the romantic sound of her whisper. She put the man into a trance. She bestowed soft kisses through the microphone. She boiled Frank's mind with the deep gaze of her wonderful blue eyes.

The microphone rustled over her delicate body, moved from her mouth, over her breasts, and then lower and lower. She tucked it under her T-shirt, causing Frank's violent erection of manhood, and the first sounds of the instrument plucked from the speakers were plucked by the swollen cock caressing the strings.

Vibration in the microphone, activated by guitar tones, gave spice to caresses. Sliding it between her legs, Kari was caressing her femininity.

They were getting closer to each other. When they were at arm's length, she tucked the microphone even deeper between her legs. She squeezed her thighs tight. She gripped the guitar with her hands. She started playing a melody using Frank's penis. She played with the sounds in the rhythm with which she wanted to be caressed.

After an exciting moment, she pulled the guitar from the male shoulders. In return, she handed the microphone and hugged it to her partner's face to hear all the sighs that he gave when caressing her lips. She gently hugged and stroked the whole of Frank's taut genitalia with her hand. She toyed with every centimeter, which drove the man crazy. And it was clearly heard from the loudspeakers - from the slightest sigh to the loud scream of pleasure she gave him.

She kissed a fat cock. She caressed, harder and harder. She pressed against him more and more. The man dug his fingers into her hairstyle. She answered by scratching his ass. She sucked the penis deeply. Frank knew how she loved to move him in her mouth, just like in a vagina. He held the girl tightly by the hair. He penetrated deeper and deeper Kari's mouth. Suddenly he extended the phallus so that Kari's agile tongue would not trigger the shot too quickly. He complimented the phenomenal nature of her body.

He helped the straps of the shirt slide gracefully down her bare, smooth shoulders. He revealed the firm, spherical beauty of her breasts. He caressed, kneaded, stroked and rolled protruding nipples in his fingers. He provided a woman with amazing experiences. He hypnotized by touch. It was reaching her breasts with his mouth. His hands were directed towards her back. He ripped, scratched, made circles all over their surface. He penetrated the pass between the buttocks with delight. Kari was pushing his head down. She demanded caresses.

He kissed the belly obediently, then took care of the navel. He kissed it and licked it on each side. He crossed the strip of the rolled petticoat on his hips. It got to female deliciousness. At the same time, he felt the girl playing with his protruding manhood with her feet. She held the phallus tightly and rubbed it. He loved her closing his face in the velvety embrace of her thighs.

She teased him. She didn't let her tongue slip into her wet vagina.

He had to fight and get her millimeter by millimeter to deserve this pleasure. The pleasure of giving pleasure to your wonderful woman.

He struggled for a long time. He licked, kissed and caressed the areas around Kari's sweet triangle.

She finally succumbed to the pressure of his lips and hands everywhere on her firm, sexy body. She caught the man's neck with her thighs and wrapped it around it, igniting the senses in an embrace.

He grabbed her ass like a bowl. He held her plump buttocks with his fingers and began to drink the nectar of her femininity. He kissed delightful area around. The circles of kisses tightened. He was reaching inside. He sucked her harder and harder. He licked deeper and deeper the woman's damp shell. He swirled and his tongue raged in her like in a centrifuge. She screamed louder and louder. The whole apartment was shrouded in the sounds of emotions engulfing the girl.

She loosened her grip. She bent down. She pulled the man's head out from between her legs and pressed her lips to his. She lifted him from her lap with a kiss and tossed him on the couch. He collapsed, obediently relaxed.

Only his penis was stretched. He towered with his hardness. He moved with the waves of pleasure, stimulated by the caresses of Kari, who raged around the crotch.

Her eyes followed the protruding dick. Predatorily she stroked men's thighs, abdomen and torso. She threw her breasts at him and tapped mercilessly. She caressed him with them. It felt like a vagina. The girl let him go. She bit her lip and watched his penis sway from side to side. Hard, raised by her caresses, unaware of women's traps.

She jumped on him. She stuffed herself deeply with her whole self. She captivated the penis with her pulsating lust. Mercilessly subdued with a mad gallop. She moved her hips side to side and made circles. Frank caught her bouncing breasts in flight. He squeezed them and watched with mistaken eyesight at the female madness.

He caressed her body. He was floating. Once he cradled her lips with his lips and kissed her burning body, she would turn over and kiss him again. Only when she felt like it did she let him take the initiative. She vigorously dealt with tough manhood. She knocked a man down, dominating him with her femininity. She was jerking off a hard cock and it was delivering unbelievable pleasure.

As he felt her close, he squeezed her plump bottom in the vice of his strong male hands. Kari was scratching his torso, screaming even more. She squealed with all her might along with the sofa. The girl's breasts like cannonballs wreaked havoc on a man's mind.

The madness of the female hips drove him to the shot. He felt Kari strain. She dug her nails into his torso, bit his neck, and screamed as he exploded inside her.

He wrapped his arms around her, hugging her tightly against him. He vigorously moved under her so that the still tense, large cock still caressed her vagina enjoying her orgasm. She loved it.

To be continued...

I'm happy you read the first part of my novel
I will also be happy if you tell someone else about my novel